I0621075

DEDICATION

For everyone who ever felt they don't matter and no one cares. You are wrong! You *do* matter and there is *always* someone who cares. Mostly I dedicate this book to my friends, Mark Shepherd, Vivian Williams and Saul Tweedle who just didn't understand that. Their deaths left holes in so many lives. There is never a good reason to kill yourself, so just don't do it.

Permanent Solution to a Temporary Problem

Selina Rosen

JUST CAUSE

An imprint of
Yard Dog Press

Permanent Solution to a Temporary Problem
Selina Rosen
First Edition Copyright © Selina Rosen, 2019

Published at Kindle under "Just Cause,"
an imprint of Yard Dog Press

This is a work of fiction. Names, characters, places, and incidents are the products of the author's imagination or are used fictitiously and are not to be construed as real. Any resemblance to actual events, locales, organizations, or persons, living or dead, is entirely coincidental.

ISBN 978-1-945941-18-4
Permanent Solution to a Temporary Problem
First Edition Copyright © Selina Rosen, 2019

All rights reserved. No part of this book may be reproduced in any form or by any electronic or mechanical means, including information storage and retrieval systems, without permission in writing from the publisher, except by a reviewer, who may quote brief passages in a review. Any members of educational institutions wishing to photocopy part or all of the work for classroom use, or publishers who would like to obtain permission to include the work in an anthology should send their inquiries to Yard Dog Press at the address below.

Yard Dog Press
710 W. Redbud Lane
Alma, AR 72921-7247

http://www.yarddogpress.com

Edited by Selina Rosen
Technical Editor Lynn Rosen
Cover art by Melanie Fletcher

First Print Edition June 1, 2019
Printed in the United States of America
0 9 8 7 6 5 4 3 2 1

TABLE OF CONTENTS

AGGY MAINSTREAM

"What are you doing, trying to get kicked outah school?" Sam hissed in a whisper.

"No one's gonna know but us," Virginia said, closing the sack and rolling the top closed.

"Where'd ya get it?" Aggy asked.

"My dad...."

"You stole a gun from your dad," Aggy whispered, "are you fucking nuts?"

"He'll never know. Besides, I might just blow my brains out and then it won't matter."

"Ah, come on, Virgi...." Aggy started.

"Man, you're the one who says life isn't worth living. How come when you want to blow your brains out you got a reason, and when I want to, I'm being stupid..."

"Or melodramatic," Sam said. "Let me see it." He held out his hand.

"Not during class... maybe later."

"You three have something you'd like to tell us?" Mrs. Gram looked down on them from the end of the long table they sat at in study hall.

Aggy had seen her grandmother in her casket. They had put all kinds of makeup on her to try and make her look like she had when she was alive, but somehow it just made her look all the more dead. The ravages of time had not been kind to Mrs. Gram, and a more enlightened person would have seen a pathetic woman trying desperately to hold onto her long-lost youth, but Aggy was sixteen, and all she saw was a corpse trying to look like a living human.

"Just working on our homework," Virginia said without a hint of guilt, and Mrs. Gram took her word for it in spite of the fact that they didn't have a book between them.

1

Aggy's heart was in her throat.

"You've got to learn to lighten up." Sam laughed.

It was easy for him to say. He didn't know what it was like living with her dad. Her dad, a man that everybody—even Aggy—loved, and who could turn from a loving, tender man into a raving lunatic in three seconds flat. Very little that Aggy did was right, and it was her fault that he beat the shit out of her. After all, she was a screw up, a disappointment.

Life in her house had always been a roller coaster of emotion. Her dad had all the power, her mom didn't know whether to shit or go blind most days, her brother and sister were perfect, and she was the whipping boy.

"Don't give me any shit," Aggy hissed at Sam.

"Chill man," Sam said with a smile. The bell rang. "Let's go to the store and get lunch."

It wasn't a long walk, and it was a nice day. They bought a couple of sandwiches. Virginia lifted a couple of bottles of orange juice and they walked between the store and an old gas station to eat so Sam and Virginia could smoke a couple cigarettes, which was way cool.

There was only a three-foot gap between the buildings. Sam was puffing on a cigarette and playing with the derringer.

"Don't let anyone see it," Virginia said. "My dad would kill me..."

"Thought you were gonna kill yourself, anyway."

"Maybe I will," Virginia stammered out.

"Shut up!" Aggy screamed. They both looked at her. "You're fucking pissing me off with the gun thing. Just put it back in the sack and we'll take it and put it in your locker..."

"Just listen to Miss Death, would ya? When there's nothing ta do it with, Aggy's gonna kill herself every ten minutes." Sam turned away from them. When he turned back around he had the gun in his mouth.

"Sam, no!" both girls screamed. Sam pulled the trigger, then laughed. "Ah, come on, you don't really think Virgi had the guts to load it? You girls are a lot of talk. He threw the gun to Virginia and she quickly put it in the bag. They had a good nervous laugh. And then they busted the bottles against the wall because they were mad at the world and started back to

2

school because they hated their lives but didn't yet know how to break the big rules.

It had all happened a hundred years ago, or at least it seemed that way to Aggy as she looked out the window of the plane at endless blue and white. It was so peaceful you could almost forget... almost. It all seemed so unreal. Just yesterday they had been kids and now...

"Thanks for coming with me, Aggy. I don't think I could do it myself, and I really didn't know who else to call... No one else here really knew Sam." She started to cry.

Aggy put an arm around her shoulders and ignored the stares they got from the other passengers.

"What made him do it?" she sobbed. "What makes someone kill themselves?"

Aggy swallowed hard. She would have liked to be able to say that she didn't know. Except that she did. In Aggy's life she had asked herself "why live?" many more times than "why die?" Life was hard when you didn't fit in, when you weren't mainstream. People put you on the outside and made you stay there then called you fringe or worse things. They used you and when you wouldn't put out any more, they threw you away.

The friends you made in your youth, those true friendships became the victims of time, distance, and responsibilities, till you rarely even thought of them. You forgot their birthdays, and then you even forgot to send them a card during the holidays. They rarely crossed your mind—till they were gone.

Eve straightened herself and dried her eyes. "I'm sorry."

"It's all right." Aggy looked out the window.

"You know, I can't even remember off hand how old my own brother was..."

"Thirty-five. We were all the same age."

"That's right... You know I always thought you and Sam would get married," Eve said.

Aggy laughed and shook her head. "Sorry to disappoint you, kid, but we never got any further than kissing..."

"Why not?"

"No chemistry." Now that was a good, safe answer one that didn't out either of them.

"I hadn't seen Sam in a year. What with the divorce and all... well, it's just been a shitty year." Eve started to cry again, but made herself calm down. "The last time I saw him, he and Amy seemed so happy. I thought he finally had his shit together."

When someone said you had your shit together that meant that you had given up on any of your dreams coming true and settled for the crumbs that life had to offer. You were doing what was expected of you, succeeding on everyone else's terms. Aggy swallowed a harsh response.

"The last time I saw Sam was at Virgi's funeral two years ago. He seemed ok." It was a lie; he had been absolutely miserable. Forced into a life he hated, married to a woman he loved but in the wrong way, with more bills than he made money. He had just been buying everything he thought might make him happy and of course none of it ever did. "We made a pact to stay in touch, but we didn't. Maybe if I had reached out and picked up the phone—made an effort, but you get to the point where everything just seems so futile." *Like maybe your brother has the right idea and I'm the one who's fucked up, because his life couldn't have possibly been any worse than mine is. Every day is pain, and nothing I do makes me happy, and no one really gives a shit. There have been days ...nights where if I had called Sam—or anyone for that matter—and they didn't have time for me, it would have just been too much. And I would have been the one eating a gun. So I played it safe. I didn't call. I don't let anyone in, because I know they only want to use me and hurt me. Or worse yet they'll never live up to my expectations and it will just be one more thing that sucked.*

When they finally realized that it really wasn't going to get any better. When all their dreams had been murdered by reality and responsibility, they blew their brains out. Now Sam's sister—who doesn't remember how old he was and hasn't seen him in a year—gets me—who didn't have time for him and who he didn't have time for—and together we scrape up every dime we have to go and see him put in the ground and what's the point of this? What is the point of any of it?

"We had grown so far apart." It was all Aggy could muster.

But we hadn't changed at all, and neither had the bottomless pit within us that nothing could fill. We were still those three kids

4

playing with that stupid gun because we were all scared to death to just be us.

"I wonder why that happens. Why people just drift apart?" Eve asked, letting the tears roll down her face.

Because you have to go out into the world and get a higher education or go to work, and then you have to find a meaningful relationship, which is a fucking joke because if they love you and you don't love them then you live in guilt and if you love them it's a sure bet that they won't love you unless they can make you over in their image and while they're doing this you die inside and everyone says, "He finally got his shit together."

"I guess it's just part of growing up."

Eve wanted to change the subject, and Aggy was more than ready... "Do you still write?" ...for any subject except that one.

"A little." *Five or six hours a day in between a full-time job I hate and trying to figure out why my life is such a piece of shit.*

"Did you ever have anything published?"

So why don't you just give me a gun and then all three of us will be dead. "I sold a couple of short stories." *Nothing that got me any prestige or any real money, just enough to make me think that I might make it, a taste but not the real deal. Like everything else in my life, the glass isn't half empty it's all the way empty.*

"That's cool." Eve took in a long breath. "What are the chances that... what are the odds? First Virginia and now Sam." She shook her head. "It just seems so odd that they both killed themselves."

About as odd as three hockey players all having blade scars. The thing that brought us together in high school was that we were outcasts. Weirdos that no one wanted to play with. All of us were gay, none of us could admit it even to each other but we knew. We were unhappy kids and we grew up into unhappy adults. Go figure.

"I guess it is pretty weird."

"I'm not looking forward to seeing my mother." Eve sighed. "She's a slut, you know."

If Aggy had offered any comment it would have been too much. "Slut" was the nicest thing she could think of to call Sam's mother and Eve had already used that. Eve seemed to be tired of talking and Aggy was just as glad. She gazed back out the airplane window down at the earth below. It was so pretty from up here, but down there it was dirty and people didn't give a damn about other people, and there hadn't been room for Virginia or Sam, and there was no place for her.

The service was held at the gravesite in the rain and led by a preacher who had never met Sam and thought he was going straight to hell because he had killed himself. She had to walk away from the service to keep from telling him where to stick his sermon.

The rain poured off her head down her shirt and into her jeans, and she was still happier to be out here walking amongst the head stones then back there under the leaky tarp listening to an asshole condemn one of the best friends she'd ever had. Looking at the wife who was crying more from guilt than grief, and watching his whore mother grieve in between trying to play grab-ass with the boyfriend of the week was more than she could take.

And they wondered why Sam had killed himself. They acted like it was some great mystery. Hell it was a wonder he'd lasted as long as he had. A miracle he had killed himself before she had—frankly she probably had more reasons than he did.

"Why the hell not!" she screamed back at them, even though she was sure she was too far away to be heard. She walked around until she decided she'd better get back to the service. Too late. Not only was the service over, but everyone was gone. Somewhere, between grief and the rain they had forgotten all about her and left her here at the cemetery alone. She walked over and sat down on the coffin, which no one seemed to be in any hurry to plant. Water ran off of her and onto the coffin.

"You don't mind, do ya, Sam? Hell, no one's gonna be seeing this fucking box again, a little water stain won't hurt." She was alone and she let go. Her tears flowed in a steady stream till her body was shaking, her nose was running, and she felt like she was going to puke. Then she tried to stop. She didn't know how long it took her, but it was starting to get dark, and no one had come back for her.

"So. This is it. Sooner or later this is where you end up. Fat or thin, rich or poor, happy or unhappy. You live a useless, futile life filled with crap. You work your ass off trying to make your dreams come true and in the end you die and they plant you in the ground. If there is a hell, I don't think you're going there, my friend. Killing yourself isn't evil. It just cuts out the middle man. If there is nothing but pain—if this is really it—what cruel bastard would make you live? I can't even say I'll miss you, because I haven't seen you or even talked to you in years. I'll miss what we meant to each other, you me and Virgi. We used to talk about killing ourselves. Me more than either of you. I always thought it was because I was more afraid of what I was, but maybe not because I'm still alive.

"It was always just talk. The way we tested each other to see if we all still cared. It was so good to hear that you mattered to someone, anyone. And we would talk about what we wanted to do. How we wanted to change the world and make people stand up and cheer when we walked by. Somewhere in the back of our minds we even believed all that. We lived in Shitville, and we were all going to get out. You and Virgi did; but I couldn't. I never did, and I guess that in fact, neither did you. Maybe if we had grown up anywhere but a small town in the South, we might have found acceptance. But once you get it drilled into your head that you're the problem, that your wants and your needs are stupid or sick... Well, it's hard to believe anything else.

"I always thought you guys were going to get what you wanted. Remember the one time I tried to lift something? I got caught. You guys did it every day, I did it once and they caught me. Remember how we used to break bottles between the buildings? Well here's a secret for you, one I never told anyone. I used to go back later and clean it up. You guys smoked—I never did. You always used to gig me about being such a tight ass, but I just couldn't let go, so I stayed out of a lot of trouble that you guys got into. But I lived in fear, and I always knew that I was a disappointment to everyone even though I was trying so hard to be just what the world and my family wanted me to be. And doing that—trying to—well, the person I have disappointed the most is me.

"So, here we are. Me alive and you dead, and I think I'm safe in saying that you're a hell of a lot happier than I am. Since you'll be worm food soon, you'll even be more productive than I am. You always were so competitive.

"Well, you've turned into a lousy conversationalist, and it looks like no one is going to come back for me, so I'm just going to mosey on down the road." She got off the coffin and started to walk out into the rain. She stopped and turned around. "Bye, Sam. Be seeing you soon."

It always came down to this. She didn't want to hurt anyone's feelings. She would always get this close and then she would think about how upset her parents and her brother and sister would be, and how they would probably blame themselves, and she just couldn't do it to them. No one gave a crap about her now, but just let her kill herself and suddenly everyone would decide she was the most important person in their lives. She'd seen that—heard it—at Virginia and Sam's funerals. She put the gun down on the hotel table and looked at it. She had gone to a great deal of trouble to get it and it had cost her all the money she had brought with her—plus her plane ticket home.

"I've just got to do it. Just like Virgi and Sam. I can be as tough as them." But she didn't want to do to her friends and family what Virgi and Sam had done to her.

Murder. Murder couldn't be blamed on any member of the family, and people got murdered in Kansas City all the time. In fact, there was a dark alley just outside the hotel. She put her jacket on, put the gun in her pocket and left the motel room. As fate would have it, Eve and her mother were leaving their room at the same time.

"We were just coming to get you," Eve said. "I'm really sorry we left you in the cemetery yesterday. Since we have to fly out in the morning, I thought you might let us take you to dinner tonight."

"I'm... I'm not hungry, thanks anyway," Aggy said.

"Then where are you going?" asked the whore of Babylon.

"I thought I'd go on a little walk," Aggy said quickly.

"In this neighborhood!" the tramp screeched. "Why, that would be like committing suicide."

Eve started crying, and while the "mother thing" was trying to explain her poor choice of words, Aggy made her escape.

The alley was dark and she smiled at how perfect it was. They hadn't had enough money to stay in one of the better hotels in the safer part of town, so they had made do here in scumville. She walked to the end of the alley and stuck the gun in her mouth. Then she decided that her clothes should be torn—like she'd been in a struggle—so she torn them up some. Then the gun went back into her mouth. But no that was going to scream suicide. She was going to have to shoot herself in the heart. She put the business end of the gun against her chest.

So this is it. In a minute I'll be dead, putting an ending to the meaningless misery of my life. If only I could have made a difference. If only I had found someone who cared more for me than they cared for themselves.... I'm stalling again. I want to be dead. I just don't want to have to do it. Maybe part of me believes all the crap that preacher was saying about my eternal soul being damned, but... I don't really believe any of that shit. I believe you die and you're worm food. Since that's the case why should anyone live in pain? I'm tired, sick to death of the constant stream of shit that runs through my life. But maybe I could just be me, maybe I could just finally live my life and not worry about what anyone else thinks. Dead's the worst thing you can be right? And I could kill myself, I'm standing here ready to do it and... I could always do it later if life doesn't get any better.

It wouldn't get better because if she just did what she wanted there was going to be a lot of fall out and could she really deal with that? Would it be better or worse? She couldn't do worse; she just couldn't. She hated the life she had but was afraid to do anything different because she just couldn't do worse. But if she was willing to die to get away from the life she had, why not give it one more try?

Suddenly there was a loud noise, and three thugs pulled a fourth man squirming into the alley. There was a gleam of steel—one of them had a gun. In that moment things seemed quite clear she pulled the gun away from herself, aimed and fired. When she quit firing, the three would-be hoods lay on the ground, and the victim looked at her, obviously wondering if he was next.

"Damn, I can't even get suicide right," she mumbled.

The near victim got up from where he had fallen. "I thought I was a goner! At first, I thought I was just going to get mugged, but when they drug me in here... You just saved my life. Thank you."

"No. Thank *you*." Aggy walked up to the man and smiled. She wiped the prints off the gun, dumped the rest of the bullets out of it, put them in her pocket and dropped the gun close to the hand of one of the guys she had just killed. "I'm getting the hell out of here; I suggest you do the same."

He nodded and took off running.

She walked quickly out of the alley and down the street. She didn't know where she was going or what she was doing next, but it was going to be different. She knew she should feel something besides excitement. She had just killed three people and maybe she would feel regret later, but right then she just didn't and she knew why. She had been about to kill herself so killing a bunch of thugs wasn't such a big deal. *I wish I could talk to Virgi and Sam. I'd tell them you don't have to kill yourself. You can just walk away from being you and be who you want to be and if it sucks too... You change everything again. I'm not going home.*

IT WASN'T MY FAULT

I remember that day whenever the weather is cold and grey with a light drizzle that appears to want to drive the light from everything. Today is a remembering day.

There had been a time when she was my hero. When I was a kid, before I knew the wrongness of her, she was my everything. Then like everyone else I pretended to accept her but mostly saw her the way they all did—as someone beneath me—because you see Brenda was a lesbian. It was 2012 and we lived in the South, so while I had gay friends and thought I was cool with it the truth was just like the rest of my family. I thought I was doing Brenda a big-assed favor just allowing her in my space, not spitting at her or calling her names because of course she had dealt with that her whole life.

That and then some.

It had been a cold drizzle, one that soaked us but wasn't enough rain to make us blow the whole thing off and go home. We stood there as a family and watched as her wife scattered her ashes across her yard as she wanted. My grandmother cried, her wife cried, and the little guy, her grandson he cried like he might never stop. It wasn't his fault at all. His parents were the ones that took him away from her; he was still little and like I had when I was a kid, he idolized her. No one else shed a tear. Not me, not my mom or my sister or my aunts, uncles or cousins. No, we were all just way too busy trying to decide how Brenda's death wasn't really our fault. Her son—my cousin, but so much older than me I really saw him more like an uncle—just stood there and snarled, occasionally telling the little guy he was going to be alright, which was a lie. We didn't know it then but none of our lives were ever the same after that.

You can't remove the light from a family and have anything, anything at all but darkness left. When someone kills themselves there is guilt and remorse and no fixing things ever

11

again. We bullied her to death. She wasn't a teenage kid; she was a woman in her late fifties, so I think we just didn't think she could do anything like that. I know I never thought she could.

It wasn't my fault. On days like today when I can't stop thinking about it that's what I tell myself—except it *was* my fault because what I said to her was the last straw. See there is a tipping point to everything including how much pain one soul can carry on their own and she was always and forever on her own. People everywhere and they all wanted something from her but she... Well she was always on her own; no one helped her.

She had come to fix a bunch of things that had broken around my grandmother's house. She was already walking the razor's edge, and if I'd had any soul or compassion I would have known that, but I was nineteen had been living with my grandmother since I was sixteen, pretending that I was deeply depressed because my mother had basically left me to be raised by my grandmother. How terrible was that? I went from having rules and being treated the way I acted to having no rules, being given a car and having someone take my side every single time I was wrong. I hadn't graduated from high school—all the school's fault was what I told anyone who would listen. In those days everything happened *to* me; I never owned any part of what my actions caused. That day my aunt Brenda was running around fixing everything I had watched fall apart while I played computer games and made dishes and dirty clothes for my grandmother to wash. Not really proud of that; it's just the truth.

I got worried that my grandmother might finally hear what Brenda was constantly telling me and my grandmother—that I was the one who should be doing all these things—so I got up and decided to cut down a tree that was brushing the house. I decided to cut it five feet from the ground and in a place that would have me whacking my machete into the side of the house behind it. Brenda of course just had to come and take over. The whole time she was chopping on this tree I kept saying it should have been cut where I started to cut it, so finally without a word she handed me the machete and started packing her tools.

Well I cut at that tree and banged my machete into the house a dozen times taking hunks of the siding with every chop and then it bound up, but finally it came down. As she was

12

walking to the truck with her tools, I just had to rub it in her face, "Hey I got it." She roared out of the driveway, spinning gravel.

When she called my grandmother later my grandmother took my side—as she always has. She told Brenda I was a good boy and that I was just trying to help her and she needed to have some patience with me. That was the tipping point for Brenda— that one thing that was just too damn much.

At the actual memorial I didn't really feel guilty. Like everyone else, I came up with a thousand reasons why it wasn't my fault. No words were spoken; no one had anything to say. The little guy cried; his father didn't. Her son was too busy being mad. Why mad? Because Brenda being dead made the little guy cry. And my cousin knew, he *knew*, that one day the little guy would figure out that the reason his grandmother was gone was at least in part because his parents decided to move him so that she could hardly ever see him and she needed him because he was the only one who really cared about her. See you can love people a hell of a lot and not care about them a diddle shit. My cousin is a good guy of the white hat variety. He loved his mother, and he was mad at her because he blamed himself. He knew how attached she was to the little guy; that boy was her whole world. When they moved to another state and she went from seeing him every day to the prospect of being lucky to see him once or twice a year it was more than she could really take. Her heart and her spirit were broken. But I hadn't cared about any of that, all I had cared about was that she was threatening my comfy lifestyle. So, I also loved her but didn't care about her.

As kids we all loved Brenda. She was funny and bright and she always treated us like we were the only ones in any space. She made play houses and castles and tree forts all over her place for us to play on and in wonderful places that built your imagination. She made up games and played them with us. She told us stories and took care of us when we were sick, and we all loved her until it became unpopular to do so. I think that's what she couldn't take; that the little guy was going to grow up and be just like the rest of us. That he was going to grow up and then he wouldn't choose her either.

That's what I tell myself when I begin to believe it was all my fault. None of us want to accept our part in "it." None of us want to own what happened to Brenda, not her wife, not her son or my grandmother me or anyone else. We all used her, all of us. We used her and then basically treated her like crap and someone else's—anyone else's—feelings were always more important than hers because other people would get mad and be vindictive or they'd stay mad and not talk to you, but Brenda, maybe because we all made her feel so worthless, always put up with our shit till the day she couldn't anymore.

Someone would do something horrible to her, she would get mad, then she would blame herself for feeling anything because after all *she* was what was wrong. Even when she and everyone else knew she was dead right. It didn't matter because none of us—not one of us—had her back. We expected her to make nice because we knew other members of our family were not capable of admitting they were wrong about anything.

We made her eat shit, but worse than that we expected her to act like she enjoyed doing so.

Even when we weren't abusing her, we let other people do so. She meant nothing to us till she was dead and we had to do all the many things she did for us and... Why would she hang around to do that? Why would anyone hang out to be the family whipping boy so that they could do all the many thankless tasks the rest of us thought we were too good to do?

That's the worst thing we did to her. We discounted her to the point that she had no self-worth at all. She did amazing things trying to prove her worth, but we always treated her like crap so she never believed she was enough. No matter what she accomplished she felt like she was running in a deficit. She wrote books and plays, she acted, she painted, she sculpted, she could build anything. It's true she never succeeded at anything; at least nothing she did ever made her any real money, but she did them anyway. It should have been enough and it would have been if we hadn't all knocked ourselves out to make sure she knew everything she did sucked. See we needed her to believe she wasn't really good at anything because otherwise how could we justify making her drop all the things she wanted to do to take care of our shit?

Joseph Campbell said, "Follow your bliss." Brenda tried. She might even have made it if she didn't feel like she had to take care of all of us. But she felt like she had to because the only time any of us were ever even nice to her was when she was doing something for us.

If she couldn't make us want her, she would make us need her and we did. We didn't really know it, but we did.

Her wife served a meal. To this day I don't remember what it was or if I ate or not. They talked about stupid shit really—their jobs, yard work they wanted to do, maybe they would buy a new car, what grades the kids were making and why.

My grandmother had stopped crying and so had the wife. The little guy had a room at Brenda's house where he went and got his toys. Once he had those he quit crying. Kids are like that; they can shift gears really easily.

As I looked around Brenda's living room which was no longer hers and watched them all talking about themselves and what they needed or wanted to do, I clearly heard and understood Brenda's words for the first time.

It happened three days after my tree cutting triumph. The family got together at my grandmother's house for someone's birthday I don't remember whose. When Brenda got there, it was obvious to anyone that she had been fighting with her wife. Her son wasn't there so neither was the little guy. They had already moved out of state—he had a job or something. Most likely his wife just wanted to stick it to Brenda as hard as she could. See Brenda made her look bad because she did the things with the boy that his mother should have been doing but didn't feel like doing because it didn't serve her.

I was of course still mad at Brenda because she dared to be mad at me because I had acted like a huge human turd. But everyone could see she was in a mood and they were all sort of steering clear of her—even her wife was. She was having trouble coping with the new Terrible and we all knew it and didn't care. Our problems were real; hers were made up. It was the first time she didn't rise above whatever problem she was having and make a party where there was none. She wasn't running around entertaining us, so we all just sort of sat around making small talk and eating huge gobs of calorie-rich food pretending like everything was alright. Pretending like we liked each other.

Pretending there wasn't a giant gaping wound caused by abuse in our family, and it was easy for all of us to pretend as long as Brenda was because most of the abuse had been heaped on her.

That night she was beyond pretending and she couldn't even start to do or say things just to make us happy because in that moment she cared about us the same way we cared about her— which was not at all.

The "party" was super boring just like every single get together we've had since Brenda died.

A couple of one of my other cousin's kids were there and when they ran over to play with Brenda and she didn't even look at, much less engage with them, I knew something was badly wrong. So, did I feel for her, did I reach out to her, say I was sorry? Or even just give her a hug? No, I got super mad because I thought she was still mad at me and what right did she have to be mad at me? She was the one who did something to me.

In righteous indignation and doing something I never did, I addressed everyone saying, "Did you see I cut down that tree that was rubbing against the house?" I looked at her, daring her to say anything, anything at all but she was already beaten at that point. So, did I shut up? Give an apology? No, when she failed to rise to my challenge I said, "You were wrong, Brenda. My way was just fine; I didn't need your help. No one actually needs you."

Everyone got real quiet like maybe they knew the shit was going to hit the fan. Then Brenda turned and looked at me and the anger I expected was not there, just deep all-encompassing sadness.

"Yes, Golden Boy. I do everything here while you sit on your ass and do nothing, then you finally get up and do something that didn't really need to be done in a way that did more harm than good and let us all applaud."

My grandmother who is more than soft spoken said in a near whisper, "Now Brenda calm down." My grandfather beat Brenda and my grandmother never once even asked him to stop, never gave Brenda comfort afterwards, never dared to tell my grandfather that what he was doing to Brenda was wrong. But me she defended.

And that broke the rest of Brenda.

"That's right. Because I'm the problem. Isn't that everyone's go to? That I'm what's wrong."

"We should just go," her wife said.

I don't think that would have changed anything except then we wouldn't have heard what she said next. We could have separated ourselves further from what she did. We could have continued to pretend.

"Why because I'm making everyone uncomfortable? How about this... You all make me uncomfortable... how about that!" She looked at my grandmother and lowered her voice. "Just once, just once choose *me*. Just once I want to be the one who can do no wrong. I want someone to have my back. You let Dad kick me and stomp me. From the moment Kerry was born I didn't exist except to be her whipping boy. You chose her over me and Dad over me. No one, no one ever chose me. I'm always at the bottom of everyone's list if I'm on it at all. You all worry about how everyone else is going to feel and never once consider how I might feel."

"That's not true. Let's just go," the wife said.

"It is true. You chose your worthless, drug-addled daughter over me. You let her turn my son against me which wasn't hard to do because his worthless fucking father already had. He never chose me. None of you, not one of you fuckers ever thought about what I needed or wanted. I'm the first one you call when you have a problem but the last one you consider. I feel like my guts have been pulled out and stomped on and do any of you actually care? Do you call just to check on me, bring me a cake, something, *anything*... No, I never hear from any of you unless you fucking need something. My therapist says I must learn to love myself, but how can I when the people who should love me don't and never have. When you all seem to go out of your way to kick me when I'm down. I'm down, all the way down. I can't see even a drop of light, so just keep kicking, don't stop, kill me and get it over with."

Everyone was quiet then, no one said anything till I—still sure that I alone was the injured party—yelled, "Why don't you shut up and go home!"

"You..."

She looked at me then, and this time there was so much anger in her eyes that I knew her soul was filled with rage. I was

17

scared shitless. I could feel my blood pumping through my heart carrying a wave of cold.

"You want to play the big hero, the one who saves everyone from my meanness. But in order to be a hero you have to do something besides nothing. I took care of you, I spent money I didn't have on you, and time I could have spent doing something of worth. Yet you have no regard at all for me just like the rest of them. Not one of you has ever given me a damn thing, not one of you has ever put me first. You have worn me out doing all your crap and none of that has bought me even an ounce of affection much less respect. You win, alright? You finally win. I can't fight it anymore. You're all right; I'm a worthless piece of crap. I cause all the problems in this family—me, me alone. I cause all the problems in your lives. Everything is all in my head. I cause my own pain."

Her wife tried to leave with her, but Brenda didn't let her go. She walked out the door and into the woods so far we barely heard it. In fact, it wasn't until hours later when she didn't come back and we couldn't find her and the cops did that we realized that we had all heard the shot fired. She put a gun to her head, but we all pulled the trigger.

And all of us died a little that day. We had all loved her. She was the fire in our family and we doused her light not to raise ourselves up but only to keep her in a position where she would have to grovel to us. We made her think she needed us, but we all needed her. Maybe that's the real reason she did it, to make us all suffer, but she's dead so how did that work for her? You know what she should have done? She should have lived—really lived. Told her old lady that they were moving closer to the little guy and her son and she could go or stay. She should have left all of us to fend for ourselves. You know what she shouldn't have done? Killed herself. Because now she doesn't have any chance at all to make her life what she always wanted it to be. It's like she left a painting half-finished and now no one will know what it might have looked like.

None of us were ever the same. We had no idea what she did for this family, the hundreds of different things she did that made our lives not just easier but more worthwhile, that everything she said and did was only to help us be better people. Her being gone didn't make me a better person. It left a hole in me and in everyone who loved her but never took the time to actually *care* about her.

Except for the little guy, none of us thought we needed her. Her son sure didn't, he thought she had ruined his life and was right in the way of him having what he wanted. It was the main reason he moved, or so he had told her. He moved he said because he was tired of her meddling in his life. Though as far as anyone could tell, her "meddling—as it was with most of us— was him making a huge mess and her cleaning it up. She's gone and her son didn't move back. His mother being dead didn't make his wife any less of a bitch, it didn't fix all his problems, it only made the little guy cry. Now her son knows what he lost, but when she was alive he couldn't get rid of her fast enough. If she hadn't killed herself maybe just being away from her might have made him realize how much he loved and needed her. Maybe he would have moved back and then she would have had the little guy again and everyone would have been happy, but she stupidly ruined any chance of that. My cousin has never even been back to visit. I think the rest of us... Well we just remind him that his mother is gone. Seeing us just rekindles his guilt.

She killed herself; it didn't fix anything. It left a sad, hideous mess and most of us are just mad at her for doing it. She didn't win when she killed herself, but we all lost.

There are a new batch of kids now. They are mostly nasty little plastic people. They have never known the joy of someone looking at them with a love that can be felt. They don't know what it is to go on an adventure, or fight monsters. All the things she built have fallen into ruin because her wife pays some guy to take care of the yard and he does a shitty job. Brenda's widow seems like less of a person now, not from sadness but because without Brenda her widow is just sort of there. My grandmother's place is falling in around our ears. She still makes excuses for me and I still make them for myself.

We killed Brenda with our disloyalty and disregard. We never cared how she felt as long as she just kept it to herself. If she had died in an accident we would all feel worse than we do, but because she killed herself we blame her for the fact that we unloved her to death.

None of us ever defended her or helped her. We kicked her when she was down and whined that we had been injured if she dared to complain about the way we treated her. NO ONE EVER CHOSE HER. When push came to shove, she always got pushed back in favor of someone else. Always someone much less deserving.

It's not all my fault. It may seem like it but it wasn't. She had the gun in her pocket the whole time, and she had already written the note. We all had a piece in killing her. Maybe, maybe I own more of it than everyone else because I just had to be a douche bag. But why did I think it was alright to treat my aunt like that? Because everyone else treated her that way. No one cared a diddle shit about how she felt. I talked to her the same way everyone else did.

How fucked up is that? We drove her to suicide yet none of us want to take credit. We all want to say, "Not my fault." Some of them even blame me; it's easy to do because I was the last one to treat her like shit.

There was a note in her pocket. The cops gave it to my mother's other sister who read it out loud.

"They say that suicide is the most selfish thing a person can do... I am finally doing something for myself."

People always want to judge the person who kills themselves. They are selfish or crazy or just trying to hurt their loved ones. Probably all of those things are true, but why are they doing something so selfish, why are they crazy, why do they want to hurt their loved ones? The truth is Brenda killed herself because she couldn't stand the pain anymore. She didn't have people who loved her—at least not in a way she could feel. Except that little boy and they used him to do possibly the worst thing that was ever done to her. They used his love for her and hers for him as a way to torture her. They took the best thing in her life, the thing she counted on, and they made it into a nightmare.

And did the rest of us reach out to her? Were we there for her, did we try to help fill the void in her life? No. She was right. We just kept right on kicking her when she was down.

There is enough blame to go around. All of us have blood on our hands. We all loved her but never showed it in a way that she could feel. We all needed her but never thanked her with more than casual words. We showed our whole entire asses whenever we felt like it and expected that everyone would just pretend we hadn't done so, and none of us ever paid for blowing up and throwing a fit. But Brenda wasn't allowed to even have an opinion, to defend herself, to even have a bad day. We made her pay for any small sign of bad temper because after all she was a queer and we were really great people just because we let her be around us and didn't call her a pervert to her face.

I owed her everything; I gave her nothing but crap. I didn't kill her. I refuse to take the blame. But I helped to make her think that death would be better than the way she was living.

In *Murder On the Orient Express* they *all* kill him. They each go in and stick a knife in him. That's what we all did to Brenda every time we chose someone else over her. We all did it. She said it and it was true—no one ever chose her.

In the end she did it to herself, and really who knows why but the truth is she never should have done it. That little boy loved her and even if she only saw him once or twice a year... Those would have been the best times of his life. He didn't get that and he needed it. I might deserve for Brenda to be dead I was a shit head, but the little guy he was just a kid and she robbed him of even a little bit of time with the greatest playmate a kid ever had. I wish I had never started seeing her any differently than I did when I was a kid, wish I hadn't let the whispers of my adult family and my friends at school get into my head and had just accepted her for who she was—a wonderful woman who loved with her whole heart who just wanted to be loved back.

Today I will walk out to the woods. To the spot where her blood soaked into the ground where the cops found her with her limp hand still around the gun. Her face twisted in the torture of a life half lived. I don't know if there is an afterlife. If there was a G-d, surely that G-d would protect people like my aunt Brenda from people like us—not give her a family that made her live in hell on earth.

I will go out there and sit and look and wonder, but nothing will bring her back.

Mostly I will sit and convince myself that it's not my fault. Maybe this time it will stick.

THE CRYBULLY

He was young, he was pretty, he was wildly popular on line. In truth, having never dealt with any real problems or come up against any real prejudice or abuse, he found every single thing he didn't enjoy to be a personal affront. He was a product of the victim culture who had "G-d sucks!" tattooed on the front of his neck, and on his arm in big block letters below his short sleeve shirt it said, "I hope I am so hated in life that when I die people throw a party."

He was well on his way to having his wish.

He pretended to be offended by any number of things yet wanted everyone to let him say and do whatever he wanted and if they were offended… Well then they were persecuting and discriminating against him. He tore them a new one on his blog. In fact, to that very date Marcus Imacribbe had never actually confronted anyone face to face to accuse them of the crimes he fried them for on line. No, he sat safely—and usually a half a country away—and lobbed insult after insult and accusation after accusation of his abuse at people who had no idea they had offended him at all till they read about it on line.

He got paid to whine on the internet. It was a pretty sweet gig. His blog was very popular and embraced completely by a culture of other crybullies who near worshiped him. Every single mistake anyone made in his presence was seen as the most horrible sexual harassment, racial slur, or homophobic attack. His followers ate it up at the same rate a chemical toilet ate shit. In truth, he thought everyone was an idiot—especially his followers.

He had ruined people's reputations, their careers, and their lives, and he was damn proud of the fact. It made him feel important and powerful. Now one of his rants had driven someone to suicide. Far from being apologetic, he had been in the middle of writing how Tara Franks had killed herself because she couldn't defend her objectionable actions when she suddenly showed up at his shoulder.

"Yes, that's nice. It wasn't enough to kick me when I was down. No, now you're going to slur me in my death. You really are just an unbelievable douche bag. How stupid was I to care at all what an ass hat like you has to say?"

Marcus spun around in his chair and looked up. She didn't look like a ghost, so he reached out and his hand went through her. For a minute he thought maybe it was just a guilty conscience, but when he searched his mind he found didn't feel guilty at all. In fact, hearing she had killed herself made him feel completely and totally excited—like he had the power of people's life and death at his fingertips. When he said as much, his boyfriend stomped out of the house having a sudden need to visit his mother.

"Wow... you just really lack even an ounce of compassion for anyone else don't you," she said. "Of course, how could you possibly have any compassion left over for ANYONE else when you use it all on yourself? It must be hard to be so completely sensitive; how do you live with it? I was really sensitive, too. I didn't show it, but I was. I guess that and not because..." She looked beyond him to his monitor and read, "...I couldn't defend my objectionable actions, is why I killed myself. Because I was walking a razor's edge of sanity because of the very real abuse I have lived through. Then you accused me—a gay woman—of sexually harassing you. In the middle of all the crap you 'me-too-ed' me. How very brave of you. You drug my name through the mud and tried to ruin what I no longer had anyway—a career."

"What are you doing here?" Marcus asked.

"What do you think I'm doing, dumb fuck! I'm haunting you." She found a chair and sat down. "It wasn't really my idea. Apparently, something—maybe that G-d fellow you think sucks—decided I didn't just get to be dead. That's all I wanted. I just wanted all those voices in my head to quit telling me how wrong and worthless I was. I had shut them up so many times, but I was already having trouble when you decided to slur my name on your blog over what one might argue was a tasteless joke. But certainly I—a gay woman who had dealt with hell because of men—would never sexually harass you or anyone else. I told myself I wasn't going to read any of the four billion tweets from your mindless army of biting virtual ants, but I did.

"Worse yet, I was told by people who 'cared about me' that my only recourse was to apologize to you or ignore the whole thing but that I should not—under any circumstances—defend myself or call you out. So I did apologize but apparently yet more public humiliation wasn't good enough and I sat there day after day as I watched your minions take one pot shot after another at me as you carefully deleted any post that defended me or my actions. You made sure there was only one side to the story—yours."

"You're dead. It wouldn't have killed you to give me a real apology. I really did feel threatened by you."

"Dude you're forgetting I'm dead and I have to tell you being dead I know things I didn't know when I was alive. You might as well know that lying to me is a huge waste of your time—not mine. I'm dead; I got nothing better to do. You didn't feel threatened by me at all, you were never uncomfortable. You wanted the panel to be all about you and what you thought. I did a joke, they were all laughing with me, you couldn't stand not being the center of attention; it's as simple as that."

"Well..." Marcus didn't really have any idea how to defend himself when someone knew the truth. "Why did you have to be the center of attention?"

"Why do you think, mother fucker? Oh, I can call you mother fucker, can't I? I mean since you're a gay man that just shows that I'm mad, not that I'm actually being a homophobe. Well of course I can. Why does anyone need attention? Because it's a form of acceptance, a form that being a gay woman now in my fifties and dead I never really got. You have no idea what I've been through—a father who beat the living crap out of me for everything and especially tried to beat the gay out of me. An abusive husband who used me in ways I can't bear to talk about even in death. At least when people were laughing at me I knew they didn't hate me. I knew they saw me. And the people in that room, most of them, were my friends, my fans, I did the joke for them to make them laugh—which they did. I didn't do it to make you uncomfortable. I did it because for a minute I needed to feel the love of other people. It was never about you, you self-important mother fucker, and by the way I think you can only get really pissed off if you are a mother fucker. I mean isn't that your game? Everyone picks on you because you're gay. Because you're ethnic... by the way what race are you since... well to me you look white."

"My great-grandfather was from China."

"And my grandmother was Cheyenne Arapaho. I didn't think every time someone used the term Indian they meant it as a slur against me or anyone else. And you know what? Neither do you. You know damn good and well that all the many people you have slandered, none of them meant you one ounce of trouble. That's the real problem, isn't it? That it wasn't about you at all. No one noticed that you were so sad and so defeated and used and put upon, so you had to point it out. But not to their faces—never to their faces."

"I'm not the only one who thought what you did was sexual harassment, Jessy Problochi said..."

"He wasn't even in the room. But it must be nice for you to have someone always at your shoulder telling you when you should take offense and in what ways you have been mistreated. Does he get a cut of your slander money? No, he doesn't. He does it only because he thinks you're super famous—which by the way you are not. You have thousands of tweeter followers who got on your blog and picked me to pieces without knowing anything about me. You knew nothing about me and do you know what really sucks, pecker head? Wait... is that gay bashing? No, that's me bashing you because you pissed me off. What really sucks is that I liked you and I thought you liked me. I would have never purposely done anything to make you feel bad because I liked you and because—unlike you—going out of my way to make people feel like shit just for being who they are... that was never me. That's what literally killed me. The fact that I thought you were a fellow human being just trying to make it in this fucked-up society the way I was. Further because you were also gay I thought you understood me but I was a fifty-eight year old woman from the South, and you're a twenty-five year old snot-nosed kid raised in New York City. You lived through made up persecution and sexual harassment, while me—I went through the real thing. I dealt with real hate, real abuse.

"But you surprised me because until you did your little dance of hate I never in a million years would have thought anyone—much less you—could think such things of me. But I should have, shouldn't I, because what had I learned over and over again from my life? That everything I am is wrong and that people will always attack me because they can. I notice that you have never, ever gone after any writer or actor who had enough fame and money to sue your ass off. No, it was always someone like me. Someone vulnerable."

"I only go after people who go after me."

"Liar!"

He jumped when she yelled at him.

"You're a fucking liar. I didn't go after you and you know it. Meanwhile how many times did you turn off your ultra-sensitivity when it was someone with a big name and money and fame? Then you aren't sensitive at all, are you? Try writing something like you did about me about one of the big shots... You won't do that will you because you know damn good and well the mega corporation that funds your hate mongering smear..."

"I'm standing up for human rights..."

She laughed then, and the hair stood up on his arms.

"You're making yourself rich and famous. I know what it means to stand up for human rights. I marched on the capital past the lines of people in sheets with their swastikas and confederate flags screaming 'G-d hates queers!' I called state senators, I lived my life in the open at a place and time you have never known. You are complaining over bullshit and... well you want to be as offensive as you can be and cry persecution if anyone dares to say they're offended. Then you want everyone to watch every single thing they say or do in your presence, but wait! That won't work either, will it? Because you are just *looking* to be offended. There is no staying out of the line of fire because you make your living being a crybully. Without people to slander, to point the finger of prejudice and racism and homophobia at, you don't have a following or a job. Someone like I was—a huge, over fifty, loud dyke—I was such an easy target, wasn't I? Wasn't I!"

27

When she thundered this into his ear he jumped and nearly pissed himself, and the smile of satisfaction on her face told him she was happy about it.

"So, piss-ant punk, what's it like to have to deal with actual harassment? How does it feel to be really attacked?"

"Why are you doing this to me?"

"When in doubt go into victim mode. Wow! I'd like to act surprised. Boo hoo, boo hoo, no one understands me, everyone picks on me, why me?" she cried. "Fuck you, douche bag. I'm dead because of you. I'm dead because I had dealt with a lifetime of bullies and you did exactly what had always been done to me... No wait, everyone who had abused me to that point at least had the integrity and the courage to stand toe-to-toe with me and beat me or rape me or tell me that I was an abomination. You waited for months and then attacked my character, my personality, on line like every other keyboard cowboy. You turned your minions on me and you didn't care at all how it made me feel. How it affected my nearly already nonexistent career, my friends or my family. You certainly didn't give a good G-d damn what it did to me. No, you had Jessy and all your fans chirping in your ear telling you how wonderful and magnificent you are. How brave to come forward and defend yourself and point all these haters out by name."

"It's not my fault you shot yourself."

"Says the man who was apparently traumatized because I did a joke he didn't like. A man so sensitive that every single thing said in his range of hearing must have been a direct attack on him. You got on the internet and as much as called me a pervert. It *is* your fault I killed myself because your crap and the crap of your 'followers' was the straw that broke this camel's back."

She poked him in the chest with her finger then and he could feel it, so he tried to touch her again but there was nothing but air. She grinned down at him where he still sat in his chair because he couldn't make his limbs work. His blood ran cold, and she hissed in his face.

"Yeah, that's right, mother fucker. I can touch you, but you can't touch me. How's that feel? How does it feel to have someone attack you while you are completely powerless against them?"

Marcus couldn't speak; all he could do was cringe.

"Because of you, because you just had to get even for the *nothing* I did to you, I did a stupid-assed thing that left my wife and my kids to wonder why they weren't enough to make me stay here. I fucked up, and now I'm stuck with you. That's right, mother fucker, you heard me. I'm stuck with you. My family didn't understand that I just couldn't live in that space any more, not with the pain of my past traumas playing out in my head, without decent sleep, with the night terrors, as I just kept getting hate mail and friends just kept telling me I shouldn't fight back that I should have known better than to do that joke."

She started crying then, and for some reason Marcus didn't really understand this scared him more than anything else.

"People attacked me. I could never fight back. Ever! I just had to take it. I blamed myself. I always blamed myself because if there wasn't something horribly wrong with me why did everyone think they had the right—even the duty—to attack me and make me feel like crap? What was so wrong with me? What?"

"You were loud and obnoxious."

She stopped crying and laughed. If anything, this was worse. She got right in his face.

"And why was I loud and obnoxious? Because I just needed someone to *see* me. I wanted people to like me, and here's what I know now that I never knew when I was alive. You were in very poor company—of everyone who actually knew me only a hand full of people thought I was obnoxious. I was loud, but that didn't bother them because it turns out that—while I never accepted it no matter how much and how many people told me—I was very well loved. But see I never believed any of those people. No, I always believed ass hats just like you."

"I really don't appreciate the way you are cussing me and putting me down."

"Wow! Did you find a backbone in those pretty boy togs of yours? What about touching you in a sexual fashion? I mean after all we're here alone I could do that. Hell, I can do anything I want. I don't care what you think did happen, let me assure you that I would never do that to you or anyone. Here's a big clue for you, ass hat, I don't give a flying fuck what you appreciate. Though you and your followers will never believe this, the world does not revolve around your hypocritical ass. You are a flash in the pan; enjoy your fifteen minutes of fame because it's all—every bit of it—about to come crashing in on your head. Every one of the people who told me to let you get away with murdering my character..." She reached over and hit the send button on his computer... "...when they read this none of them are going to be quiet anymore. If I had to do it over again, seeing what my wife, kids and friends are going through, I wouldn't kill myself because now, only now do I know how much I was loved. I was loved so much that what you said, what your followers said, shouldn't have mattered at all. I should have just clung to those who really knew and loved me and blown you and your hate mongering minions completely off. I think it's so ironic that your own words are going to fry you."

"I can delete that from my page," Marcus said.

"Really? Because I sent it to MY friends list."

"No one cares about you!" Marcus screamed.

"Yeah, that's what I thought, too. Turns out we're both wrong."

He watched for hours as the hate mail came in. Not only did people care about this nobody, but many of them were really well-connected, and one of them was hugely famous and had buttloads of money. They had already threatened to sue the corporation that funded his blog and by six o'clock he waited for his boyfriend to come home from visiting his family and collapsed in his arms crying.

"What's wrong, Marcus?" he asked.

"Tara Frank's ghost is haunting me, and I lost my job. Even some of my followers are saying I went too far this time. I might get sued. It's a nightmare, a terrible, horrible nightmare."

His boyfriend looked at him and frowned. "What are we going to do for money?"

"What?" Marcus asked in disbelief. "I was haunted today. I lost my job. People—lots of people—have been really mean to me."

"I told you, Marcus. I told you that you were going too far. How are we going to pay the bills? And if you get sued..."

"Wow! That's got to sting like shit," Tara said at his shoulder, eating an apple. "What's that like? People smell blood in the water and it's a sudden feeding frenzy, they are calling you names and threatening you, and him..." She laughed. "He doesn't give a crap about you. No, he's here for the free ride. Here's something you might want to learn right now; people can only care about you as much as you are capable of caring about them. You are using him, and he is using you."

"She's right there, do you see her?" Marcus pointed at the ghost.

Raymond looked at him like he thought he was on crack. "The woman's dead. You went too far and somebody a lot more sensitive than you pretend to be is dead. You forget I met her; she was friendly and funny. You have not an ounce of remorse. Why do you think I spent the day at my mother's, Marcus? The woman killed herself because of your post and this morning you were gloating about it. Gloating like you were proud of yourself. It's sickening."

"Fuck you, Raymond! Get out! Get out! Get Out!"

As Raymond shrugged and went to the bedroom to pack his bag the ghost laughed in his ear.

"That's who you are, isn't it? You do things to other people and they're supposed to take it. They do something to you and they're supposed to eat shit... Well who's eating shit now?"

"Leave me alone!" Marcus cried, bending over and holding his ears.

"No can do. No, this is my job now, to torment you. All these years you've been acting like you're treated badly for a whole line of stuff that were mistakes at worst. Now you're going to find out what it is to have a real problem, to have someone... well thousands of people really truly not just wishing you ill but actually doing bad things to you. All those people, faceless people that you don't know, spewing hate at you and for what? You were just being yourself... Doesn't irony bite?"

Marcus hardly even noticed when Raymond stomped past him with his bag and slammed the door. He guessed he'd be back for the rest of his things later.

"How am I going to pay the bills?" Marcus muttered.

"That's a good question. I guess you'll have to get a real job, one where you will have to break a sweat just like all the jobs I

31

ever had because I never made a living writing books and I always had to work some crappy hard-ass job just to pay the bills. Nope, I never caught a break as sweet as the one you had."

"This isn't fair!"

"Yes, it is. This is the first thing that's ever happened in your entitled lucky-assed life that is fair." The apparition laughed again, slinging her head back. "You want to hear what isn't fair? What you did to me and everyone else you slandered. When you killed all those people's careers how do you suppose they paid their bills? That's what's not fair."

Marcus walked back to his computer and flopped in the chair. There were hundreds of Emails and Facebook tags. As he scrolled down not one of them was from his followers. None of them were defending him now.

"This is all your fault."

"Really? Because if I hadn't showed up you wouldn't have sent that message?"

"I wouldn't have sent it to your friends."

She laughed loudly. "No, I don't guess you would have. You're probably right; if your shallow, air-headed followers had seen it first they would have been all about agreeing with you, but now that there is a huge shit storm with some very rich and famous people all calling you a human turd... Well, they don't want any part of that, do they?"

Marcus turned back to the computer and quickly typed, "Look, I did not write that. I had a fight with my boyfriend. He wanted to hurt me and he wrote it."

"Yeah, go ahead and send that," the ghost said reading at his shoulder. "That just might work. But let me tell you something right up front. If it does work, the universe is just going to find another way to get its pound of flesh, you know. Or I will because it doesn't look like I'm going to be going anywhere soon."

He sent it; things calmed down. Another benefactor picked his blog up for half of what he'd been making. Tera's friends had even mostly quit attacking him. But he still wasn't getting the hits he was getting and as he sat there trying to think of something to write he found that every single time he almost thought of something he was afraid to write it because of the repercussions.

"And how's that feel?" the ghost said at his shoulder.

He almost jumped out of his skin because she hadn't been there since that night and he was sure she had moved on.

"Excuse me?"

"How's that feel? The whole being afraid to write anything because anything you say or do might come right back to bite you on the ass? Seriously doesn't that just make it almost impossible for you to leave your house much less write something?"

He sighed. "It doesn't feel good," he admitted.

"You got so full of yourself, so full of your own worth and your feelings that you discounted the feelings of everyone else. And someone like me who's so loud, so out there, I couldn't possibly be sensitive or broken or have any feelings at all. Certainly, I couldn't have friends and loved ones who would miss me."

"I'm sorry."

"No, you aren't. You aren't sorry you did it, you're just sorry I'm here bugging the living shit out of you. Now you have to pay for what you did. And isn't that nearly exactly what all your little followers said about my apology? Know what? They were right. I was only sorry I did it because it caused me all that grief because unlike what you did to me... I never meant to hurt anyone. No, you aren't sorry at all. In fact, you blame me for everything that's happened to you. But you will be sorry; I promise you that you will be."

Her laughter could be heard long after she disappeared. But he knew now she wasn't really gone. She had said it; she was stuck with him.

A cold chill ran through Marcus and he shivered. He looked at the screen and could think of nothing he could write that might not tick someone off not if they were as "sensitive," as he was.

He hadn't read any of the books he was supposed to or done any of the reviews. The new company he worked for had asked him NOT to make public appearances until the smoke cleared and without going places where people could do things he could take offense at, what did he have to write about? He was losing more followers daily.

"Boo fucking hoo, poor Marcus, everyone hates him, no one loves him, he might have to eat worms." She now talked to him three or four times a day. Sometimes he would wake up at night, roll over, and there she would be.

"Leave me alone! Just go away," he cried, holding his hands to his temples.

"Would if I could, but as long as I'm stuck here... As long as I am miserable, I'm going to make sure that for once in my life I don't suffer in silence."

"Do you want me to kill myself, is that what you want?

"Seriously, I don't care one way or the other. Not if I have to be stuck with you. But I have to tell you I wouldn't count on killing yourself as a way of getting away from me. Near as I can tell being dead means you don't have a whole lot of choices. Of course, in life I never really had choices unless you can consider bad or worse choices."

"Just exactly what do you want from me?"

"I don't think what I want matters a diddly shit. My guess would be that the Universe wants you to feel something for anyone besides yourself. They want you to actually feel sorry for all your crap, but just like I know you don't, so does the Universe... or G-d or whatever you want to call that thing you don't believe in."

Then she was gone but she wasn't, and Marcus decided to go on a bike ride just to try to collect his thoughts. He was just riding past the alley when a huge hand grabbed him and jerked him into the shadows so quickly his bike kept going for a few feet before it fell over. He was slammed up against a wall by a mountain of a man and a gun was stuck mostly into his nose.

"Do you know who I am?" his attacker asked.

Marcus shook his head quickly and silently.

"I'm Tara Frank's son. That's right. I like seeing that fear in your eye; it should be there. I've traveled across the country and waited for weeks for your pathetic chicken shit ass to walk out of your hole."

Marcus started to scream and the big man cocked the gun.

"I love my mother, but the truth is till she started living with Tera we never knew whether we were going to get three square meals a day or where we were going to sleep. Not because Mama didn't try, but because our daddy ran off and didn't help at all. Mama got with Tera and I'll admit I was a little shit at first because who wants to be the kid with two moms? But Tera, she made sure we always had a safe place to live, regular meals, and she was always good to us and our mother. She was going through hell—things she had buried in her mind came up and she had to deal with them. She had PTSD so bad I don't think she had slept in months, but she insisted on going to that convention and you killed her. She thought it was going to help her get out of her funk, and instead you killed her."

Marcus was sure he was dead, but then Tera's ghost appeared at her son's huge shoulder. "Jimmy, you stop. Jimmy!" The big man's finger moved off the trigger and Marcus breathed again. "Jimmy, don't do this. You won't be able to live with it. I'm so sorry baby, so, so sorry. Please."

"Listen to your mother," Marcus pleaded. "Listen to her. You don't want to do this."

"Listen to my mother... You bastard, my mother is dead." Tera was jerking on the boy's hand, and Marcus realized that the man could not see, hear or feel her. She was his ghost; she was haunting him. She couldn't affect anyone else. That was her curse.

"Please, Jimmy, please." Jimmy uncocked the gun, so maybe on some level he knew she was there.

"You ever read one of my mother's books?"

"No," he answered truthfully.

"If you had you would have known she could never ever do what you accused her of. That just wasn't who she was. She had been through such hell that she was just always kind to everyone. Her biggest problem was that she assumed everyone was as open and loving as she was. She never saw the worst in people until it was too fucking late. All she ever wanted was to entertain people, to be accepted, but she never was—not by people like you." He cocked the gun again.

Tara's ghost freaked out. "No, Jimmy! Please, Jimmy!" Then realizing this was getting her nowhere she looked at Marcus. "Tell him you're sorry. He doesn't really want to do this. Tell him you're sorry."

"I'm sorry, I'm sorry," Marcus said.

Again Jimmy uncocked the gun, but he still didn't move it out of Marcus's nose. Marcus wondered why the street outside his apartment building had to pick now to get so damn quiet.

"You're going to have to do better than that. He has it in his mind that the only way he can honor me is to kill you," Tera said.

Marcus didn't look at Jimmy; he looked at Tera. "I really am sorry, truly sorry. I was completely full of myself and incapable of seeing anyone else's pain. So in tune to the things I found offensive and sure I was doing the right thing and fighting for a cause that I forgot that there were people whose lives I was affecting in negative ways. The truth is I was so busy being incensed that I just didn't care. I am really, truly sorry. Please, I know there is no way I can bring your mother back, but I knew her well enough to know this: she loved her wife and her kids and her friends, and if she had been in her right mind she never would have done this to any of you, but she was walking the razor's edge and I pushed her over. My only defense is that I didn't know how bad she was. Just like she didn't know I was so easily offended."

"Tell him you know this isn't what I'd want for him," Tera coached.

"You know this isn't what Tera would want you to do. You know that she wouldn't want this for you. She wouldn't give a shit what happened to me and why would she? But she would never, ever want this for you."

The man removed the gun and let go of Marcus. It was only then that he realized he'd held him against the wall off his feet all this time. This guy didn't need the gun. Jimmy started crying and put the gun in his pocket. Tera tried to hold him, but she really couldn't, and for the first time in his life Marcus understood that everyone's feelings were just as important as his. That everyone was just as important as everyone else.

"I really, truly am sorry. I just didn't know and I didn't think."

"Just get the hell out of my face, you bastard!" Jimmy hissed.

Marcus was only too happy to oblige. He grabbed his bike and quickly rode home. As he walked into the apartment carrying his bike, Tara was sitting on his couch.

"Sorry about that. The boy's always been a bit of a hot head," she said.

Marcus nodded and rubbed at his nose. "When I was sure he was going to kill me I thought, she's right I am sorry. But then... when I realized what he had lost. What I had caused him to lose. Then I was really and truly sorry. I know it's too little too late..."

"Not for we dead people. I think... I think maybe now I can cross over or whatever."

"Really? Because I'd kind of like to get to know you now," he said. "I need something to write. I'm blocked. I'd like to write about you. To find a way to apologize for all the harm I've wrongfully inflicted and maybe find a way to stand up for myself without walking on other people."

"Well... I am a really good writer."

"You dictate; I'll type."

WELL, THAT DIDN'T GO AS PLANNED

He wasn't sure just what he had expected, but it wasn't this. He looked down at his crumpled, emaciated body, at the blood splatter on the wall, and the gun in his hand.

He was still in pain. Apparently, that didn't go away, but here came his fourth wife and his son from his third marriage running in and they were screaming and crying. He grinned; this was more like it.

His son was crying and saying, "He just couldn't stand the pain anymore."

His wife saying, "He always was a good man. He just wanted to make it easy for us."

But then he started to hear what they were thinking. His son was thinking, *This is my fault. He knew taking care of him was causing me problems with my wife and with my job so he killed himself.* And that was great. That was just what he wanted.

It was what his wife was thinking that threw him for a loop. *That hateful bastard is finally dead. No more keeping him here because he wouldn't go to a nursing home or into hospice. His son will finally get out of my house and I'll never have to deal with Steve's shit again because he's finally dead. No one will.*

"I just don't know what I'll do with my life now," she said, but she was thinking, *Have fun, dance on his fucking grave. As soon as his body is cold, I will give this boy Steve's 'private' journal in which he brags about every hideous thing he ever did to anyone. I will pretend like I never read it and give it to the boy and then... there will be no one living that will remember him with anything but hate. Which is all he deserves. Rest in hell, you hateful bastard.*

Steve didn't like hearing what was in her mind, and he didn't like her plans at all, not at all. He was a master manipulator; he had used and abused people his whole life. They deserved it because they were all stupid. Committing suicide was supposed to be his ultimate manipulation. He got cancer which sucked and he kind of knew it was the universe making him pay for all he had gained in life by using others, and he used the cancer for years to guilt people out of their money, to guilt his son into jumping through hoops for him. Hell, he had taken every dime he could get his hands on and gone on one cruise after another just to make sure there would be no money left for his son to inherit. With the cancer no one would ever say anything but that he was brave. He hadn't even really felt bad till that last month because he had always loved drugs and now he could get all he wanted and eat all he wanted. Then he got his son to come care for him and he spent the whole four weeks the boy was wiping his ass and hauling him around acting like he was out of his head and just filling the boy's head with a whole bunch of lies and half-truths to make sure the boy would hate his mother at least as much as Steve did.

And why did Steve hate his son's mother? For the same reason he hated all his ex-wives—they dared to get tired of his abuse, tell him how they really felt about him, and leave him.

The plan was to leave all his "survivors" in the bottom of a pit none of them would ever be able to dig out of, not make him the villain in all their stories.

No problem; he would just go get that journal and get rid of it.

Except when he left the room and went to the hiding place and there it was... well he couldn't open the secret door pick it up and get rid of it because he didn't have hands.

The cops came. They asked a bunch of questions. One of them was a guy they went to church with, and he said comforting words to Roy and Charlian about how sorry he was and how it was obvious what happened but they still had to ask questions and file a report.

And then he could clearly hear what the cop was thinking.

That thieving bastard. He deserved the cancer. So many people who don't deserve it die immediately and in pain, but this bastard just wouldn't die. What has it been, nine, ten years since he was diagnosed? Then he got on the pulpit and cried about it and talked about how good Jesus was to him and people just kept giving him money. My dad was a good man. He got cancer and died six months later in poverty and pain, but this fucker... Well he could have taken a handful of pain killers and no one would have even known he did it, but he just had to blow his brains out to make sure everyone knew he was still in control. Every word he ever preached was a lie. He never believed any of it. When the going got tough and he was done torturing his wife and kid he does this with his son in the house... The only upside is that the bastard is finally dead. And good riddance.

The stuff in the other cop's head wasn't much better. He didn't know Steve, but he was nearly as judgy.

What kind of asshole shoots himself with one of his kids and his wife in the house? Why didn't he just take a handful of the pills that are everywhere in a hospice house? Of course, what sort of asshole has their wife and kid take care of them through this crap instead of going into a home or a hospital? I'd never do that to my kids, it's just wrong and... well look at the mess he's made in this house. No one wants to live in, much less buy, a house someone offed themselves in.... Gary is right this guy was a douche bag.

That was his name—Gary. Steve was still in pain and... well what the hell was this? Why wasn't he in heaven or hell, or just dead? Why was he seeing and hearing all this? No heavenly voices were talking to him. Except for the living he felt no other presence. Maybe it was too soon. Maybe it would happen later. Didn't these fuckers understand the rules? You weren't allowed to think bad things about people who got cancer or were dead. People who got terminal cancer... well he had been expecting to be sainted.

In the next few days as people came and went bringing more food than Charlain and even Roy—who had gone home and back to work—could eat, telling her how sorry they were, he began to realize that he wasn't really the master manipulator that he thought he was. That just because they didn't *say* didn't mean they didn't *know*. Oh, he had used them all, but they had all figured it out. They had all hated him to different degrees, none of them were sorry he was dead, and every single one of them thought he was either the worst coward or a total asshole for the way he had killed himself. The only one he had managed to make feel any guilt at all was Roy, but that was seeming more and more like a minor victory because every night Charlain went to what he had assumed was his very secret—no one would find it till way after he was dead and then everyone would know how brilliant he was—hiding spot and she would stroke his journal and always think the same thing, *When the time is right I will show you to the world.*

Why had he written that damn journal, why? Because he couldn't stand that all the amazing, awesome things he had done and gotten away with wouldn't be known. Like the crime lord in a Bond film he needed someone to know his whole plan and applaud how truly clever he was. But first he needed them all to feel really bad about how he killed himself. He needed Roy to go to his grave loathing his mother for all she had done to poor Steve and feeling guilty because Steve had killed himself to make Roy's life easier. He didn't need for everyone to know the truth when he was still alive.

But of course, he wasn't alive. However, he *was* still in pain, and he knew everything that people were thinking—which was a strange kind of hell.

Even that thought didn't seem real, nothing but the pain was quite real.

He couldn't take another minute in the house with all the people coming in, none of whom had been fooled by his "I'm a good G-d fearing man" act at all. They all knew exactly what he had done and who he really was, and as platitudes came from their mouths the words in their heads were nothing but hate. He decided he needed to be around Roy, and as soon as he thought it, he was and... well Roy was screaming at his mother. At first, he was glad he had made the change, though he wasn't really sure how it happened because so far, no heavenly, or otherwise, voice was talking to him.

Roy was mad at his mother. He blamed her for Steve's death, he blamed her for leaving Steve, he blamed her for the ten years Roy had spent addicted to drugs. In short, he thought she was worthless and stupid, which... well *finally* one of his plans was coming to fruition.

"...you were a gay woman, you left him because you were gay, how was that his fault?" Roy screamed at his mother, his face red. His mind thinking more hateful things about her than he could speak at once. It was glorious.

But Emma was calm as she said, "I was sixteen years old when my father told your thirty-five-year-old father that he could have me. Why do you think they made that deal? He always knew I was gay, and that's not why I left him. I left him because he O.D.'d, and I was just tired of all the drugs. I didn't want to live like that. I didn't want it for me and I didn't want it for you." That was all she said, but her mind was racing and it canceled out anything either of them were saying or even what Roy was thinking.

Emma's thoughts were clear and concise. *That hateful bastard, he wasn't happy to ruin my life. He drugged me and handed me around to his friends in exchange for a lid of good pot. I was sixteen years old and I have spent most of my life trying to get well. I gave that asshole twelve years of my life mostly because I thought he was my son's father, but he wasn't; he never was. Even that was a master manipulation—a big lie. I should have known; I should have known. How stupid was I? I was young and naïve. I didn't know how A.I. worked; I thought it was his sperm. By the time I knew what he had done... Well my son was a grown man and I had already let that flaming asshole have him every other weekend. And this is my reward—a son who has zero respect for me, who hates me. Who believes that I am the villain in his life story and who holds that asshole Steve up on a pillow and near worships him. He shot himself in the head to make sure everyone knew he was in control because that was who he was, and now my son thinks he's some sort of folk hero. He's yelling at me and calling me names because I have always been here. I raised him and so he blames me, and he's hurting right now and he just needs to blame someone besides Steve.*

She took a deep breath let it out and only half heard what Roy was blasting at her as she thought, *He is dead now and I am still alive, and I am living the best life I know how and maybe someday my son will see who I really am and who Steve really was. How stupid must I be to be the only woman on earth who doesn't know who her child's father is not because of anything I did wrong, but because of what Steve did to me? He was sterile. He wanted a child to carry on his legacy and he needed everyone—including me—to think he had fathered a child. He wanted a child to take care of him when he got old and sick, and without that... well I never would have had a child. I love my son even when he clearly doesn't love me, so I owe Steve thanks for that and... At the end of the day I'm glad he doesn't have that asshole's genes.*

Why wasn't Emma telling Roy everything? He was dead now; he couldn't stop her. Hell, he couldn't even pick up his own journal. Why wasn't she just telling Roy everything about how he had drugged her and then how him and all his friends had sex with her for hours, how he told her it didn't happen and she pretended like it didn't because she couldn't live with it. Why didn't she tell Roy Steve wasn't his biological father? It didn't make sense. But then he knew why. She loved that boy more than she loved herself. She would never do anything on purpose to hurt him.

She was a stupid sap, a weakling, always had been.

He didn't want to hear her thoughts anymore. He wanted to hear Roy's, but they were scattered and hers were clear. He was screaming; she was trying to calm him down. She understood that he was hurting and just lashing out. His words were wounding her to the core of her being, but she just kept trying to calm him down and Steve realized, "She's not weak at all. She's amazingly strong. I did everything in my power to break her, to make her a basket case, but she's not."

He decided he would rather be back at his house with his fourth wife, who it turned out also hated him, and all the people who came in and went out who hated him and then he was. So he decided he would rather just go sit down by the river but he didn't go anywhere and when he tried the park, the train yard, the lake... He still stayed right there in the living room with his wife and his father-in-law who was a preacher and was going to preside over Steve's funeral.

"He was a good man," his father-in-law said.

Charlain took a deep breath and let it out. "It's just us now, Daddy."

"And thank G-d for that." He laughed, and Steve didn't have to know what was in his mind because he already did. When he had met and married his fourth wife his father-in-law had been the head of a thriving fundamentalist Christian church which

Steve had jumped right into, getting baptized and immediately becoming a deacon. His father-in-law and his wife just loved him. Jacob started giving him more and more responsibility because he trusted him... Because he was a sucker.

It wasn't long till Steve was able to turn the whole congregation against the old man and then... *He* was their preacher and he started lining his pockets with their money and they... Well, he thought they were all a bunch of stupid saps but apparently they had figured him out. Oh, he was still playing some people, but... After all, he had shot himself and since their church believed suicide was a sin, those people still sappy enough for him to have been using them didn't come to the house.

"What will you say, Daddy?" Charlain asked.

"That he died like he lived—on his own terms. Let people take from that what they will. I feel sorry for Roy. He never should have done what he did with his son in the house."

Charlain smiled then, "That's alright. Roy wasn't actually his son. Nope, just one more trick he played on poor Emma." And then she told him everything she had read in Steve's journal and hearing the thoughts in the old man's mind was like listening to a mantra because with everything she told him he just thought, *I knew that guy was a son of a bitch. I knew it.*

It was the day of the funeral and still no heavenly presence had come to take him home nor was he any less present or in any less pain. He was starting to realize that being a bastard his whole life hadn't worked for him as well as he thought it had.

Jacob stood behind his open coffin. He had asked to be cremated. Why would they ever think it was alright to have an open casket funeral for a man who had shot off the top of his head? But there it was. The truth was he knew why because he had seen inside Charlain's mind as she ordered it. She was sticking it to him in every way she could and... Why hadn't she left him like all his other wives had? Only because she didn't realize what a bastard he was till she found that journal. Till then she had been as big a fool as he thought she was, and she didn't find the journal till he'd had cancer for a while and the drugs he was taking had made him careless. He had left the door open just once. She didn't leave him because he had

45

cancer and besides being a fool she was also pretty shallow. She didn't want anyone to think she would be cold and cruel enough to leave a man on his death bed... Of course no one could have guessed he would be on his "death bed" for ten years, but hey on the plus side she got to go on all those cruises. It also turned out she had hidden money from him—a lot of it—and she planned to live pretty high on the hog because she would have widow benefits and all.

None of his ex-wives were in attendance and Roy was thinking they were all bitches which made him happy but... very few people were there. Except for Roy every person there was doing everything but dancing on his coffin. They didn't come to pay their respects; they came to make sure he was really and actually dead. Why? Because for the last ten years he had made a point of telling them he knew he didn't have long left on this earth and because most of them were good people and everyone hated cancer they had dug down deep on several occasions to make his last days on earth comfortable. Some even seemed shocked that he was finally dead.

Jacob tried to have a somber tone, but he was nearly giddy so it was hard. He was just happy to have outlived Steve and his words were just words. Pleasantries... he was so tired of hearing all the pleasantries as people thought hideous things about him and he realized that no one except Roy was as blind and stupid as he thought they were. He had used them because they were trusting or naïve, but he had taught them better than that with his actions. They all knew what he had done to them and why and they hated him for it.

He tried to leave but couldn't. He was stuck there for the whole service and all the way to the graveyard and all through the graveside service, and their thoughts were a chorus of hate running through his mind that he couldn't escape. As they were preparing to leave the reception held at his house, he actually was witness to his daughter-in-law excusing herself to go to the bathroom where she smiled as big as he had ever seen her smile and then she did an unmistakable happy dance. Her thoughts were pure joy and rapture littered with a need to keep what she was thinking and feeling hidden from her husband.

He started to try and rationalize his behavior. He wasn't that bad. He didn't deserve their hate. The problem was that being dead the same excuses he had used for his bad behavior in life no longer seemed to work. He was now painfully aware that he had actually been a really horrible person.

Everyone had left but Roy and his wife, and Steve could see it in her mind that Charlain was going after the journal. "No don't Charlain! Don't do it; please don't do it!"

She didn't hear him because he didn't have a mouth. She grabbed the journal and took it to Roy. "I found this later that night when... well you know. It had this note."

Steve looked at the note. "For my son with love, your father." It was a forgery Steve had never written that but it was a good one, good enough to fool Roy which it did. "What is it?" Roy asked.

"No idea. My guess would be things he wanted to teach you but didn't have time to."

Steve didn't want to go with Roy but he did and no matter how many times he tried to leave to go someplace, anyplace else over the next three days as Roy read every word many of them two or three times, Steve couldn't escape. Steve listened to Roy's thoughts as he tried to make excuses for Steve. He listened as Roy's mind was filled with confusion and occasionally hatred and loathing.

Roy just kept reading, hardly eating, hardly sleeping, till he was reading the very last line. He read it to himself a few times and then he read it out loud. "When I kill myself Roy will blame himself, he will think it's his fault, and then he'll blame his mother and it will drive a wedge between them and... Then I win."

And with that, the last person on earth who was sorry Steve was dead wasn't anymore. And Steve was still in pain.

Selina Rosen

About the Author

I started writing at twelve as an escape. The situations I have lived through are the stuff of which my fiction is born. My relationships with the many and varied people I have come into contact with over the years is a catalogue of characters from which I pull.

I am Jewish but consider myself spiritual not religious. I have studied every form of spirituality and try to live a spiritual life. I don't always succeed, but I do try.

My wife of nearly twenty-four years and I own a small farm where I raise milk goats, rabbits, chickens and a garden. I raise—depending on the weather and bugs—between forty and sixty percent of our food mostly organically. By "mostly" I mean if it looks like I will lose an animal I will do what I think is necessary. We make no trash; we use or recycle everything.

I lived for fourteen years of my life without electricity or running water. I had my only son naturally with no drugs. Though I was married off at sixteen (in an attempt to keep me from being gay) to a thirty-four-year-old man who immediately took me to New York and stuck me in a drug den for a month, I have smoked a total of five joints in my life. I have never done any other drugs. My son was a prescription drug addict for nine years.

I have worked every shit job you can imagine from pulling car parts in a junk yard and cleaning rich people's houses to home health care. I ran an industrial plane and have logged timber using a team of mules. I have worked at saw mills, framed houses, and poured slabs. I am a carpenter and a rock mason. I can run (install) electricity, and I can plumb (I hate plumbing). I have also built more than one house using only hand tools and a chain saw. I like to hike and cave, and I love the ocean.

I fought heavy weapons (and trained other fighters) with the SCA for about twelve years. During that time I broke several bones, and I have a seven-inch plate and eight screws in my left

49

arm as a result of a bastard sword blow. Elizabeth Moon talked me into fencing many years ago and I still do that, but I sold all my armor and heavy weapons last year. Erin Grey talked me into trying Tai Chi to help with my CFS, so I have now been doing do a mixture of Tai Chi and Chi Gung every day for the last five years.

Mercedes Lackey helped me get my first short story sale in Marion Zimmer Bradley's magazine. That sale opened the door for others to MZB, one of which was included in a German-language anthology, and the royalties came in steadily for many years.

CJ Cherryh line edited the first two chapters of *Chains of Freedom* and taught me more about writing doing that than I had learned to that point.

I'm not just name-dropping here; I'm giving credit to people who helped me who certainly didn't have to. Over the years I've come to know many very famous people, and here's what I know for sure—we are ALL the same.

In the writing community the person who is the most famous and makes the most money is often the least talented or deserving—not always, but often. In our business who makes it and who doesn't is often determined by nothing in the world but dumb-ass luck. That being the case, the near worship we see of the "famous" is something I just don't get at all.

The truth is I always think bios are sort of a waste. Anyone who reads my work knows more about the real me than I could ever put in a bio. If you want to talk to me, find me on Facebook. If you see me somewhere, come right up and talk to me. I am just like you. Luckily, I have a job I love, and the reason I have this great job is that people like you let me.

About the Cover Artist

Melanie Fletcher is an expatriate Chicagoan who currently lives in North Dallas with her husband the Bodacious Brit™ and their five fabulous furbags JJ, Jessica, Jeremy, Jemma, and Jasmine (yes, they were following a theme, moving along now). When not herding cats, she turns into SF Writer Girl, and has the SFWA membership card to prove it. Her recent SF sales include "The Lark Ascending" (serialized in **Gearhearts Steampunk Glamour Review**) and "Le Gardien" (*Tales from a Lone Star: A Future Classics Anthology*, Belaurient Press). She also writes paranormal erotic romance under the name Nicola Cameron, and her second novel *Two to Tango* was just released in June from Evernight Publishing.

More Great Titles by Selina Rosen

The links provided are for the Kindle Ebook Editions.
If there is no link (yet), then go to www.yarddogpress.com and check
    to see if there is an electronic edition available or order the print
    edition.

Adventures of the Irish Ninja
The Bitter End
Black Rage
The Boat Man
The Bubba Chronicles
Deja Doo
Fire & Ice
Getting It Real
The Ghost Writer
Hammer Town
How I Spent the Apocalypse
It's Not Rocket Science: Spirituality for the Working-Class Soul
Material Things
Not My Life
The Pit
Reruns
Strange Robby
Vanishing Fame

Books in Series:

"Bad" Series (Suspense)
    Bad City, with Laura J. Underwood
    Bad Lands, with Laura J. Underwood

The Chains Series (Post-apocalyptic military SF):
    Chains of Freedom
    Chains of Destruction
    Chains of Redemption

Drewcilla Quah Books (Bawdy Space Opera):
    Queen of Denial
    Recycled

The Host Series (Evil vampires and a lesbian rabbi vampire hunter):
    The Host

Selina Rosen

Fright Eater
Gang Approval

Sword Masters Series (Epic Fantasy with lesbian protagonist):
Sword Masters
Jabone's Sword
The Burden of the Crown
The Twins

www.ingramcontent.com/pod-product-compliance
Lightning Source LLC
Chambersburg PA
CBHW030518130626
46549CB00007B/3046